THE SORRY TALE OF
FOX & BEAR

For my father, Haakon Kierulf ~ ML

For Pete, a combination of Bear and Fox ~ HV

THE SORRY TALE OF
FOX & BEAR

Story by Margrete Lamond

Art by Heather Vallance

DIRT
LANE
PRESS

Dirt Lane Press Inc.
PO Box 876, Orange NSW Australia 2800.

www.dirtlanepress.com

An abridged version of this story first appeared in serial form
in *The School Magazine: Countdown* vol. 90, June 2005.

Cataloguing-in-Publication details are available from the National Library of Australia.

ISBN: 978-0-6480238-2-1 (pbk).

Typesetting by Hannah Janzen and Vida Kelly.
Cover and design by Vida & Luke Kelly.
Produced and printed through Asia Pacific Offset in China.
5 4 3 2 1

Contents

Long ago,
far from everywhere,
someone once found a letter
stuffed into a hollow log.
It was a letter of pain and love
and anger and regret.

〜

It was a letter to a friend.

It was
The Sorry Tale of
Fox and Bear.

"'Dear Fox,' the letter began. 'This is Bear …'"

I.
The Sad End
of a Tail

We were friends, remember, when you were still around.

True friends. Close-as-can-be friends … except for one thing.

You were quick and slick and sly, and I was dumber than a pile of rocks. But that's how it was.

And it didn't matter.

Then you went and stretched the string of friendship until it snapped and we weren't friends any more.

And now you're gone, and here instead are Hare and Rooster, greedy and grinning and pushing to be my new friend.

'Fox was as mean as a spoonful of mustard,' Hare tells me.

Rooster agrees at the top of his voice. 'He made trouble as easy as cows make milk,' he cries.

Like that time in winter. Remember? With the ground frozen hard and the clouds so low they swallowed the treetops.

You were wearing your white winter coat,
and all I could see were your slick black eyes and
your red tongue.

And the string of fish you were carrying.

'What's that you got there?' I asked.

'A string of fish,' you told me.

'Where'd you get it, then?' I asked.

'I got it from—' you said. And then you
stopped. You cocked your head sideways. Your
black eyes twinkled. 'I got it from the pond,' you
said at last.

Well, that wasn't a nice thing to say, because that
wasn't true.

You took it from the farmhouse down in the dell,
where it had been hanging from a nail.

It was the farmer's string of fish, wasn't it?

But I didn't know that.

Not then.

I just wondered how you fished from the pond in
the dead of winter.

'The pond is frozen,' I told you.

I should have known—by the fishy way you

looked at my shaggy tail, and at my great winter coat, and at my poor winter ribs showing through—that meanness was fizzing through you like a dose of sherbet.

'Of course the pond is frozen,' you said. 'But even so, it's easy to go fishing. So long as you know how.'

And then you turned and trotted off through the snow, dragging that string of fish behind you.

'Can I come too?' I shouted.

'No,' you said. And you kept on trotting.

Well, the smell of that fish skating across the snow was too much for me.

'Will you show me how, then?' I asked, following after you.

'It's easy!' you said, and kept running.

'Easy for some,' I reminded you. 'But I'm not as sharp as you are.'

You stopped and turned around. 'That's very true,' you agreed. 'Follow me.'

So I followed you down through the woods and along the beck to the frozen pond.

You dropped your load and licked one of the fish
with your red tongue.

(Oh, how hungry that made me feel!)

'First you drill a hole through the ice,' you told me.

'Drill a hole?' I asked. I stared first at the ice, and
then at my paws. 'How?'

'I don't know,' you said. 'But the farmer was here
earlier, and he drilled a hole over there. Perhaps you
can do as I did, and use his hole for fishing.'

'And then what?' I asked.

'Then do as I did, and lower your tail through
the hole into the water. When you feel the fish
bite, do as I did and pull your tail out again. Simple.'

It did sound simple. I padded across the ice, lowered my tail through the hole, and waited for the fish to bite.

'Are they biting yet?' you shouted.

'Yes,' I shouted back. 'They started biting right away.'

'How many bites?' you asked.

'Some,' I said. 'More than some.'

'Wait until there's plenty,' you said. 'But only if you're hungry.'

Well, of course I was hungry. Watching you eat your fish, I got hungrier still.

'The longer you sit,' you said, 'the more you'll catch.'

You sat on the bank, and I sat on the ice. You chewed at your fish, while the fish in the pond bit my tail.

Oh how they bit!

I never knew fish could bite so hard. They bit the sides of my tail, the top of my tail and the tip of my tail. My tail burned with bites.

'I think I have enough fish now,' I said.

'I've had enough fish too,' you said.

Sure enough, there were no fish left where you sat, just an empty string.

'Is your tail heavy?' you asked.

'Very heavy.'

'That's all the fish,' you explained. 'Be careful they don't fall off when you pull them out of the water.'

'How do I do that?' I wondered.

'Take them by surprise,' you said.

Then you yawned and staggered sideways.

At least, I thought you were yawning. I thought you were sleepy from all those fish you'd eaten. I nearly yawned myself, at the thought of such a full belly.

But you weren't yawning, were you, Fox?

You were laughing so hard you could hardly stand up.

'How do I take them by surprise?' I asked.

'You must whisk them out of the water in one big *whoosh*. That's the only way,' you said.

'A big *whoosh*?' I said.

'As hard and fast as you can,' you said, and then you yawned again.

Well, I tensed my muscles, and then I sprang forward … and rolled head over heels across the ice. By the time I found my feet, you were gone. But you know what really happened, don't you, Fox? I left my tail in the pond.

Because it wasn't fish biting. It was the ice freezing my tail, and gripping so frozen tight that when I jumped forward, my tail snapped clean off!

Oh, how that hurt, Fox. It hurt like a belly-full of bees.

'What a dirty trick,' Rooster says. 'That Fox was mean enough to steal wheat from a chicken.'

Rooster should know.

'The dirtiest trick in the book,' says Hare. 'You would never catch me playing a dirty trick like that.'

'Nor me,' says Rooster. 'That Fox was meaner than a mouthful of wasps.'

Mouthful of wasps—oi! how that reminds me!

II.
A Sad Tale
of Trickery

Well, Fox, after I lost my tail I went to sleep for the rest of winter. When I woke up in the spring, I was thinner than a weasel.

I'd forgotten everything and we were friends again.

Until that afternoon when I swiped a salmon clean out of the stream and who should come trotting past?

It was you, Fox. Remember?

'What a fine fish,' you said, looking at my salmon.

Then I remembered the tail trick.

'Don't you try any of your pranks!' I growled.

'A fine fish, indeed!' you said again, careless as a gnat. 'Almost as fine as the—' And then you cocked your head to one side. 'No,' you said. 'I'm sure your fish is much finer than my—'

I should have known then, shouldn't I, Fox? I should have known, by the way your whiskers glinted, that meanness was zipping through you like lightning through a wire.

'Finer than your what?' I asked.

'Finer than nothing,' you said.

That made me so confused I didn't even notice how you kept licking your lips with that red tongue of yours.

'What's the matter with my fish?' I asked. 'Is it fine, or isn't it?'

'It is fine, indeed,' you said. 'But not as fine as the beehive dripping with golden honey that I found this morning.'

Well, how my mouth watered! Salmon is good for breakfast, but nothing beats dripping golden honey.

'Why don't we swap?' I said, quick as a wink.

And quick as a wink back, you said, 'No!'

I couldn't believe my ears. I knew you didn't like honey, Fox. And I knew you loved fish.

'Why don't we share?' I wondered.

'No!' you said.

I was so surprised I forgot all about the tail trick. 'How about,' I said, 'you let me lick your honey, and I let you lick my fish?'

'Hmm,' you said. 'I suppose that we both want the honey.'

I nodded, though you never liked honey.

'And neither of us wants the fish, do we?'
you said.

I shook my head, although we both loved fish.

'So let's make it fair,' you said. 'Whoever wins the Tree Test gets to have a single bite of the other one's breakfast.'

I nodded again, even though I had never heard of the Tree Test.

'Good,' you said, and you yawned so widely I thought your head would split.

(But you weren't yawning, were you, Fox?)

'This is the test,' you said. 'The first one to say the name of three different trees is the winner.'

Then, because you were a fair friend—and because you knew I was dumber than a troll—you sat down and waited.

You waited and waited.

You waited until you nearly fell asleep with waiting.

While you waited, I thought and thought.

I thought until the space between my ears began to hurt.

And then I had it!

'Fir! Pine! Conifer!' I shouted.

'Ash! Alder! Oak!' you shouted at the very same moment.

'I win!' I cried.

'No, you don't!'

'Why not?'

'Firs, pines and conifers are not different,' you told me. 'They're the same. I win!'

I was so muddled I couldn't tell up from down, let alone tree from tree.

And while I was trying to work it all out, you jumped forward and, instead of taking just a bite of my breakfast as we'd agreed, you grabbed the whole salmon.

Well, I may not be smart. But I can swipe a salmon clean out of the stream.

And I can also swipe a fox clean off his feet. So that's what I did.

I lashed out with my paw, caught hold of your tail, yanked you up high and shook you until you dropped my salmon with a slap.

'Not so clever now, are you, Fox?' I said.

'No,' you agreed.

'Now who's the silly one?' I asked.

'I am,' you said. 'It was silly of me to forget.'

'Forget what?' I asked.

'So you've forgotten too?' you said.

'I don't know,' I replied.

'About the dripping golden honey.'

'Oh, that,' I said.

'And how I can't fetch it if I'm upside down,' you said.

Well, my mouth started watering. It watered so badly I almost forgot how mean and sly you were. But I *didn't* forget.

'Off you go and fetch it, then,' I said, putting you down, 'while I wait here and start eating my fish.'

(See how smart I was?)

So off you ran.

And I started chewing.

Quick as a wink you were back with the beehive, buzzing and dripping with golden honey.

But I wasn't so smart after all, was I, Fox?

I was so keen to get at the honey, I didn't even
notice that the hive wasn't dripping or golden.
I didn't notice that, instead of the warm humming
buzz of bees, there was a sharp fizzing whine of …

'You dummy!' cries Rooster. 'You stuck your snout
in a wasp nest!'

'And Fox ran off with your fish!' cries Hare.

'You fell for the meanest trick in the book!' yells
Rooster.

'You must have been crazy!' cries Hare.

I try to agree with them.

And I try to forget that you, Fox, never once told
me I was crazy.

III.
The Sad Snap
of the String

Yes, Fox, I know. The next thing was nothing to get upset about. It was just a prank, wasn't it? All you wanted was a laugh.

Well, laughing is fine … except for one thing. You felt like laughing, but I didn't.

You see, I still remembered those wasps. My nose hurt, and I didn't think anything was funny. Especially not you, Fox.

But there I was, a few days later, dozing on a sunny bank. And you came along with three field mice and put them under my nose.

A little snack to surprise me with.

A gift from one friend to another.

Well, I soon woke up and saw your gift. And, even though my nose was still sore, I remembered what a fine friend you were after all.

I even forgot about the wasps.

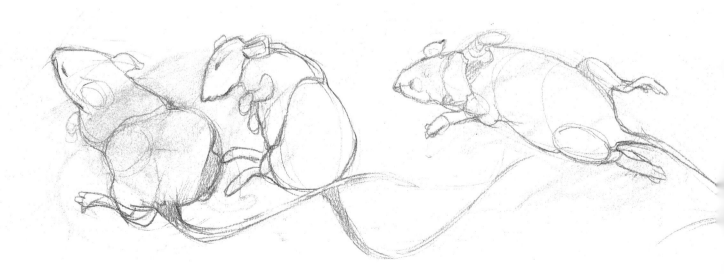

Then you yelled in my ear, 'Oi! Wah! Look out, Bear! Behind you!'

And off you ran, laughing.

How I jumped! Clean up in the air.

So high, that when I came down I missed my feet and landed on my sore snout. I scrambled up with my front paws tied in a knot, and my back legs around my ears.

And then I saw you watching me from the top of the bank. Your mouth was wide open and you could hardly stand up.

(Not yawning, Fox. Laughing.)

But I wasn't laughing. You noticed that, didn't you, Fox? You noticed me not laughing. And you noticed how big my paws were. And you noticed my sharp claws.

That's when you ran away.

I went right after you. Over the top of that bank and across the clearing and past the boulders and into the woods. You ran and ran, with your white tail-tip flashing amongst the trees. I chased and I chased, crashing through the woods.

Then I stopped. Everything was quiet.

And there was the tip of your tail sticking out from under a bush. I pounced.

'Got you!' I shouted.

Not so clever now, Fox!

But quick as a wink, you had already dashed down under a pine root.

Quick as another wink, I grabbed your back leg.

'Got you this time!' I yelled.

I held on tight, and I would have pulled you out backwards if it hadn't been for Hare.

'You've grabbed the pine-root instead of the Fox-foot!' Hare squealed, loud as can be. 'Drop the pine-root and grab the Fox-foot!'

Well, I should have known, by the way Hare's voice seemed to be coming out of the hole where you were hiding, that it wasn't Hare shouting at all. It was you, wasn't it, Fox!

But I was too angry to think. I even forgot that I already had you by the leg. So you know what happened next, don't you, Fox?

I let you go.

'*Ha ha!*' you sang from inside the hole. 'Dropped Fox-foot, grabbed pine-root! *Ha ha!*'

That made me so mad I forgot you had ever been my friend.

SNAP! went the string of friendship.

'Hide all you like,' I yelled down that hole, 'but I won't forget where you are. You'll have to come out one day. And I'll be waiting.'

Well, you did come out, didn't you, Fox?

And I was waiting.

Except that I'd also fallen asleep.

So you got away.

And I was left waiting for nothing at all.

'You should never fall asleep,' scolds Hare.

'Or listen to bad advice!' cries Rooster.

'At least not from Fox,' warns Hare.

'Only when it's us,' shrieks Rooster.

I try to listen, but Rooster's voice makes my teeth ache.

And I can't help thinking how your fur looks so much nicer than his feathers.

'But in the end I did get him,' I remind them. 'I got him so good that he never came back.'

'What a fluke that was!' says Hare.

I'm sure you remember, don't you, Fox?

Wherever you are.

It was such a smart trick.

You would have been proud of me ... if it hadn't been you I was tricking.

IV.
The Trickster Tricked

Well, after you escaped from that hole, you lay low
for a bit, didn't you? Because you remembered how
I said I wouldn't forget.

(And you were right. I didn't.)

But one day you came trotting out of the woods
and you saw me in the clearing, chewing on a bone.

You sat down beside a boulder to watch.

I kept on chewing.

You kept on watching.

I chewed some more.

You watched some more.

And that's when I knew.

I knew by the way I kept on chewing that our string of friendship was still broken.

You should have known, too, Fox.

You should have known, by the way I kept
blinking, that I was pretending not to see you.

But you didn't guess a thing. You thought
I *really* hadn't seen you.

You thought I was dumber than a pile of rocks,
same as always. And you thought you would trick
me one more time.

Which is why, quick as a wink, you suddenly
dashed across the clearing to snatch my bone.

But I saw you coming, didn't I? And quick
as another wink, I grabbed you by the leg. And
this time I didn't let you go. No matter how hard
you squirmed.

'Got you, Fox!' I yelled, and held you up high.
'Now who's the smart one?'

'You are,' you admitted.

'Why don't you get your own bone to chew,'
I scolded, 'instead of stealing from your friend?'

'Because only bears know how to find such lovely
big bones,' you said.

That's when I got my idea.

'Well, let me tell you how,' I offered.

I sounded as friendly as a friend, didn't I, Fox?

'If you put me back on the ground,' you said, 'I'll listen.'

'Oh no. You must listen in the air, upside down.'

(See how smart I was?)

'First you must find a horse,' I explained. 'Wait until it's asleep in the sun. Then tie yourself to its tail. Be careful not to wake it.'

'I see,' you said.

But you didn't see at all.

'Once you are tied fast, you must open your mouth wide,' I told you. 'Then you must bite the horse on the rump. As hard as you can. After that, the horse will be caught.'

'Easy as that?' you asked.

'Even easier,' I said.

Then I swung you around my head, tossed you across the clearing and into the woods, and went back to chewing my bone.

Well, I never thought you'd do it.

I thought you knew I was tricking.

But you thought I was too dumb to play tricks.

Oh, Fox! What were you thinking?

Of course, you know what happened next.

You fell for the stupidest trick in the book.

⌒

'*Ha haaaa! Ha haaaaaa!*' shrieks Rooster.

'*Hee-hee-hee!*' screeches Hare.

I try to laugh, too.

But all I can think of is you jolting along behind that galloping horse.

All the way across the meadow, all the way up the hill, then over the bank and across the clearing and past the boulders and into the woods and out again.

I wish I wasn't thinking of it, but I am.

'The trickster tricked!' cries Rooster. 'What a fool!'

'The prankster pranked!' cries Hare.

And now Hare tells us how he saw you.

Tied to that horse's tail, bouncing and flapping with those hoofs thumping your ribs.

Hare laughs so hard he splits his lip.

'*Aaah ha ha ha!*' shrieks Rooster.

'*Oooh hoo hoo hoo!*' howls Hare.

I keep trying to laugh.

But I can't.

I haven't seen you since, have I, Fox?

I wish it didn't make me sad.

But it does.

And I can't help wondering … where are you now?

V.
The Sad
Tale Ends

I haven't seen you, Fox, but Hare has.

Just one last time before you disappeared.

'Fox isn't as smart as you think,' says Hare. 'Not any more.'

You were still all battered and bruised from that horse, weren't you, Fox? Perhaps you'd even lost your wits.

'And he wasn't as friendly as you think, either,' says Rooster. 'Not ever.'

'Even though he tried to be friendly,' says Hare. 'Remember?'

I wasn't there, Fox, so I don't remember.

But Hare told me the story so many times I know it backwards. It goes like this …

You were lying in a clearing, letting the sun warm your bruised ribs, when Hare came by and started laughing at you all over again.

Well, of course you felt offended.

You asked if Hare was laughing at you.

Hare told you he wasn't.

'The reason I'm laughing,' said Hare, 'is because I got married this morning.'

Well, Fox! Your head was so sore you couldn't tell if Hare was lying or fibbing or just plain making it up as he went along.

So you thought you'd better be friendly, just in case.

'Congratulations,' you said, polite as can be.

'It isn't all that great,' said Hare. 'After all, it was a troll-hag that I married: claws, tail, the lot.'

Your wits were so addled, you didn't know if Hare was joking or joshing or just being plain funny.

So, to be safe, you sighed and shook your head.

'How very sad,' you said, sorry as can be.

'But it wasn't that bad,' said Hare. 'Because the hag came with a sack of gold. And a house, into the bargain.'

Well, Fox, your brain was so bruised from the horse's hooves that you couldn't tell if Hare was tricking or fooling or just plain having you on.

So you tried to look cheerful again.

'No wonder you're laughing,' you said, friendly as can be. 'Good luck to you.'

'Yeah, well,' said Hare, 'it wasn't as lucky as all that, because the house burnt down, and the gold melted and dribbled into a hole in the ground.'

You should have known, Fox, shouldn't you?

You should have known by the way Hare was shaking all over that he was laughing at you, fit to burst.

You should have known that he was joshing, joking, fibbing and fooling, all rolled into one.

But because of the drubbing you got from that horse, you believed everything Hare said.

'How terrible,' you said, regretful as can be.

'But not so terrible, after all,' said Hare. 'The troll burnt up as well and it's as if I never got married in the first place.'

Oh Fox, you should have known by the way Hare's eyes were bulging and his whiskers were trembling. You should have *known* he was up to no good.

'Which means nothing happened,' Hare went on. 'Which means I'm laughing at nothing. Unless, of course, I'm laughing at you.'

And then Hare let his laughter come flooding out all over the place, until he nearly fell over and drowned in it.

That was a mean trick for Hare to play on you, wasn't it, Fox?

It made you feel sillier than a snowman in
summer. So you slunk away with your fine bushy
tail between your legs … and no one has seen
you since.

'And now,' says Hare, 'Fox is so ashamed of being tricked by a witless old bear that he won't show his face around here, not ever again.'

'About time too!' cries Rooster.

'Good riddance!' yells Hare.

'We're better off without him!' yodels Rooster.

'He's better off dead!' shrieks Hare.

I try to agree, but I'm too busy wondering if you, Fox, ever called me witless or old.

I'm sure I'd remember if you did.

'So, what do you say, Bear?' asks Hare.

'About what?' I wonder.

'About choosing a new best friend,' says Rooster.

'A new best friend like who?' I ask.

'Like me,' cries Rooster, flapping his wings.

'Like me,' cries Hare, flapping his ears.

'Someone who is kind and thoughtful,' shouts Rooster, ruffling his feathers. 'Someone like me.'

'Someone who never plays tricks,' shouts Hare, his eyes bulging. 'Someone like me.'

'Someone who can sing,' yells Rooster, stretching out his neck. 'Just like me.'

'Someone who can leap and frolic,' yells Hare, jumping over his shadow. 'Someone exactly like me.'

'Not like that poltroon Fox!' shrieks Rooster. 'That sneak! That cad! That coward!'

'That cheat! That liar! That crook!'

'That bad egg!'

'That rotten apple!'

'Not like me!' screeches Rooster.

'Not like me!' screeches Hare.

I try to listen. But all I can hear is hubbub and hullabaloo.

I try to agree.

But all I can think is that you never once called anyone a poltroon.

All I can remember is your warm red coat, Fox, and your sparkling black eyes. Even though I tell myself Hare's fur is as soft as yours, and Rooster's feathers are as red, all I can see is flapping wings and bouncing feet.

'No,' I growl. 'Not like you.'

'Oi!' cries Rooster, jumping backwards.

'Wah!' yells Hare, leaping sideways.

And now they've gone, and I'm remembering how you and I used to be, Fox, before the string of friendship snapped.

We were true friends.

Through and through friends.

Close-as-can-be friends.

Except for one thing.

You were slick and sly, and I was dumber than a pile of rocks.

That's how it was. And it didn't matter.

But now … who is this stranger slinking out of the bushes?

It's not you, Fox.

But it almost is.

His fur is red … but dark and dirty, like mud.

His tail is bushy … but thick and prickly, like a brush.

His eyes are black … but dark and hidden, like a mask.

'I'll be your friend, Bear,' says the stranger.

He's so like you, Fox, it makes my whiskers hum.

And that's how I know.

I know, by the way my whiskers hum and my ribs feel warm, that our string of friendship is mended again.

And I know that if you came back, Fox, I'd forget everything.

'Yes,' I say. 'You can be my friend, because you're just like my old friend, Fox. It's true he made trouble easy as cows make milk. And it's true it sometimes hurt like a belly-full of bees. But that's how it was, and it didn't matter.'

But what's this?

The stranger is shaking his head.

Now he's shaking his body.

And now he's shaking himself all over.

The mud flies from his coat.

The prickles fly from his tail.

The mask falls from his face.

And I can tell, by the way you're laughing like a yawn, that you know what happens next … don't you, Fox?

MARGRETE LAMOND

Margrete Lamond loves to re-purpose traditional tales for modern audiences, injecting them with a fresh, contemporary twist. She especially loves tales that are a little bit dark, a little bit unusual, and maybe even just a little bit odd. Her books include *Tatterhood and Other Feisty Folktales*, illustrated by Peter Sheehan; *The Nutcracker*, illustrated by Ritva Voutila; and *Frankenstein*, illustrated by Drahos Zac.

Margrete is also a publisher of award-winning picture-books, a passionate believer in quality artwork in books for young readers, a researcher in neuroscience and aesthetics, and a curator who specialises in showcasing the best of international illustrative art.

HEATHER VALLANCE

Heather Vallance loves to draw animals, but not in any ordinary way. Her animals are always doing something lively and unusual, and tend to reveal secret inner selves in their faces and actions. Heather is especially interested in the way animals and people interact with their environments, and believes that the worlds we inhabit are a part of who we are. Heather shows her drawings in solo and group exhibitions. Entry into the esteemed Kedumba Drawing Award in 2016 led to her work being selected for the Kedumba Collection of Australian Drawings. Heather's art hangs in both private and public collections.

The Sorry Tale of Fox and Bear is Heather Vallance's first venture into narrative illustration.

ACKNOWLEDGEMENTS

To the tireless behind-the-scenes volunteers and
the many, many helpers, friends, supporters,
well-wishers and members of Dirt Lane Press Inc.;
our generous and super-generous backers;
our benefactors; most especially our Guardian Angels,
Freya Blackwood, and Andy and Reb McLean:
to all of you, our deepest thanks. Without your help,
be it emotional, intellectual, physical or financial,
this project could not have happened.